To order additional copies of this book, contact:
Xlibris
844-714-8691
www.Xlibris.com
Orders@Xlibris.com

ISBN: Softcover   978-1-6641-9934-7
       EBook   978-1-6641-9933-0

Print information available on the last page

Rev. date: 11/18/2021

The Tree of Sacrifice

It was a beautiful day in Shoestring City. A young girl named Faith, was walking to school with her best friend, Hunter. They lived next door to each other and that's how they became so close. Anxious to get there they knew that today their class would be going on an outing at a park for a break from the indoors school day. However, in that park was something special, something unique, it was something there that has been known to the teachers and spoken about around the students as magical called the Tree of Sacrifice. ("It sounds a little spooky but really it's not, you'll see just keep up.") To visit the tree of sacrifice was a spectacular event. The Tree of Sacrifice has been around for years. The teachers have been using it for almost forever to help students with growing and maturing their minds, like a rite of passage. So this Tree of Sacrifice was a good symbol, something ceremonial. ("Told you it wasn't scary.") Every year before graduating, teachers would take students to hang anything they wanted to show they are maturing and to leave behind something for the people to see, toys, notes, pictures of themselves on the tree, it shows that they are moving on to something bigger and better. It really was special to the students and especially the teachers, but now this is how everything went down....

Faith and Hunter, the two neighbors were up early as usual readying themselves for the walk to the school. The routine was to wait and walk with each other, as their parents instructed them to do every day just to keep safe. Both were good at following directions and were pretty responsible and didn't like letting anyone down, especially their parents. The first task for them in the morning was complete, then they reached the school.

As they entered the class to take their seats the two began a conversation.

Faith looked at Hunter seeing his face in discouragement. "What's wrong Hunter, why do you look so confused"? Faith asked?

Hunter replies. "Man I ain't confused - I don't know...I'm just nervous. Faith- "Why? Is it the trip they're planning?"

Hunter "Might be, that doesn't spook you out a little bit?"

Faith - "Not really. You've been hearing about that trip to the Tree more than I have. So why would you feel like that?

Hunter - "Yeah true. But I also heard that they were going to cut it down soon.

Faith was shocked about this and became angry because she was looking forward to the traditions that were spoken of from past generations.

Why would they do that? Faith demanded. That tree has been around for years and now you hear that it's supposed to be cut down! I don't believe it Hunter, not at all. Who in the world decided that? Where did you hear that from?

You see Faith was getting very angry and continued on with Hunter and her interrogation.   - (That's kind of a ruff way to feel early in the morning right. What do you think?)

Hunter and Faith were getting deep into their conversation when more of the class began to fill. By then two other friends of theirs had entered and noticed the talking level of Faith seemed a little aggressive towards Hunter. The two friends were brother and sister, Maddie and Mason. Now they were unaware of Faith and Hunter's conversation, all they knew was that they were there just to get through the school day. As you can see everyone was in the same class and again to be the beginning of the day, ("whew") the environment seemed a little tense. So let's see where this goes....

The Teacher....

Her name is Mrs. T.... (Uh oh ! dun dun dun dun Lights flickering on and off, thunder crashes lightning cracks) I'm kidding with the theatrics. Nothing like that.

Aright now back to the story.

Mrs. T, she is a cool teacher, easy to talk to and for some had a good sense of security and comforting aura about her, and so the students took a liking to her. Mrs. T is one who can be counted on to listen at any time, she gave feedback that was always on point but challenged your thoughts to make you challenge yourself. In other words, she pushed you to make the best out of yourself.

Mrs. T walks in greeting the class. "Good Morning class, how are we today?"

Good morning Mrs. T. - Says Faith

Hi Mrs. T.   - Hunter replied

SUP MRS. T - Maddie shouted

Mrs. T.....Yrrroooooooo Suuuuuuuup. - Mason threw that long geeting out

The four friends were the loudest and the quickest to respond and of course a chain reaction of the class began following suit with the same loud greetings just for fun.

Remember Mrs. T is a cool teacher and she knew the students admired her so even though she is a professional and had to represent decency, she liked the class participation.

Mrs. was tripping off of it, (meaning she got a kick out of the students) laughing a little under her breath and smirking.

Alright class, Mrs. T said. That was great, a little long but great. Thank you. Next time I come in here I'm going to either make my greeting shorter or be here early enough so you all have a lot more time to say hello, because I would like to begin the lessons on the same day. How does that sound? The class burst out laughing from her response because they know what kind of teacher she is and that's why they all followed through with it.

Mrs. T continues.

Class I hope we are all off to a good start as it appears but I need your full attention please and quietness. There is an announcement and I have some bad news," she said. "It's about the trip that's been planned."

The whole class quieted down, silenced like an empty room. Questioning expressions filled the class, as they waited to hear what Mrs. T was going to say. Faith and Maddie began softly whispering, puzzled because of the sudden change of mood in the room and from the teacher.

"Class," Mrs. T said as she walked up and down the aisles, "Do I have your full attention?" Now the trip that was planned today for our visit to the Tree of Sacrifice has been interrupted. Some issues have come up and the trip has been canceled. Maddie-- "Mrs. T- how come it's canceled?" Faith-- yeah, what happened?

One moment Mrs. T said--I wasn't finished; we have received news that "the Tree will be getting removed.

Hunter shouts out--"you mean cut down, Mrs. T.

Yes--Mrs. T said, "If you want to be straight forward,"

The class began to talk amongst themselves softly and very disturbed. A class of a few students quickly sounded like a colosseum of worried spectators.

While Mrs. T gave the class a moment to absorb and speak to each other on this information, one student made a statement.

Her name was Vallery and she yelled out bluntly, "Ha! they're cutting down that useless tree, It's not that important, taking up space, I'd rather be doing something else instead of hanging around out there getting bit up by bugs and having animals drop stuff on me or go through my backpack and steal my lunch! I hate when they do that, they run up a tree and tease me with it while they stuff themselves with my stuff. The class turned to vallery with a confused look on their faces.

Looking puzzled, Mrs. T herself, said, "Wait...Vallery, what...?"

Vallery didn't agree with lots of things said or done with the class. She often looked for things to talk bad about, sometimes making other classmates feel bad, somewhat like a bully. And she enjoyed it.

((Hey Vallery- not cool!))

Faith got really mad and yelled "Vallery why do you always got to say something, nobody asked you!"

Maddie jumped in-- "yeah be quiet and go somewhere,"

WHOA…. WHOA…. WHOA… Mrs. T intervened. Is this how we handle things? We know how to communicate better than this. Remember, everyone has a right to feel how they want to feel. And class, everyone has a right to not feel offended, let's be better than this and respect each other's differences.

Faith says "Mrs. T. the Tree of Sacrifice is a special part of our small section in this city. Why would they want to take it down?

Vallery, speaking very sternly and nasty, "Because no one wants it around."

Faith and Maddie were disappointed, the tree of sacrifice may have been old, but they looked forward to seeing it. Hunter and Mason were pretty quiet on the subject, and had not said a word, Faith looked at hunter's puzzled face and said we'll talk at recess. Hunter shook his head, gesturing ok.

Seeing that the class was a little unsettled than usual, Mrs. T cut for recess a little early. "RECESS!" Mrs. T projected- let's get some fresh air and break this stuffiness up class. The four friends met for recess talking about everything. Mason was in shock and hunter as nervous as he was before he was now a little disappointed.

Vallery walked by "I told you, faith, I knew this would happen, I told you so. Hey Maddie, nobody likes that tree anyway.

Mason said "Vallery this is not the time for an I told you so moment. "The tree is very old, Vallery, you have that part right." Ms. T explained. "The Tree of Sacrifice has been up as long as I can remember, it's being cut down on Friday, we will see it then."

"Why do we still have to see it?" Vallery said as she rolled her eyes. "I keep telling y'all that no one in here wants to see that old thing."

Mrs. T quickly responds to Vallery

That may be how you feel Vallery which is fine, but is that how everyone feels? I think we should ask the others in the class before a decision is made of the way everyone else thinks.

Following Mrs. T statement, you could see Faith and Maddie were disappointed, the Tree of Sacrifice may have been old, but they looked forward to seeing it anyway that year.

As recess went on, Mrs.T circled the area monitoring her class and the four friends gathered in the middle of the school yard to talk amongst themselves.

"I told you, Faith, I knew this would happen." Hunter said.

I wasn't sure what I heard was true about the Tree but now I know…. and I don't like it! We have to do something to save the Tree of Sacrifice.

Mason chimed in and said….

We can fight! When we get there we can throw stuff and yell and anybody that tries to cut it down is going to have to answer to us, that way they know we are serious and not scared. Then nothing is going to happen to that Tree.

Hunter says, "I don't like fighting and being mean."

Maddie looks to her brother Mason and asks him, "Will that solve the problem or make it worse. Do you think we can beat everybody?

We can try, Mason said! I told you, I ain't scared of nothing!

I don't like that idea Hunter said, I don't want people to get hurt especially me! I love me and I want to keep me safe.

Everyone paused and looked at Hunter with a surprised look and shouted "WHAT?" all at the same time.

(It was deep how they all answered at the same time right looking at him all confused.)

Hunter was blindsided by the response and looked around and uncomfortably said….

"What" …. Why is everybody looking at me? I don't want to get hurt, I don't want anybody to get hurt, but I don't want me to get hurt first

"We can ask people to sign a petition," Faith suggested. "That way, if we have enough signatures, they have no choice but to leave the Tree of Sacrifice standing."

"Great idea!" Maddie shouted.

So after school Mason and Hunter went around town putting up flyers with their parents in places where people could see them. Faith and Maddie took a petition and went door to door with other adults asking people to sign it and explained what the petition was about. Some people they asked disagreed to participate, saying "they wanted the Tree of Sacrifice gone, out of there, moved or obliterated". However, others agreed and said "that it should stay." At the end of the day, the four got together and faith counted up the signatures to see what progress they had made.

"It's not enough," she sighed. "We need more! We only got 28 signatures, I don't think that's going to be enough."

Hunter asked, "how many do you think we need?"

Maddie said "Mrs. T might know; we could ask her in the morning." Faith... I agree, we need some reinforcements.

Mason said.... Like more action! How come y'all not listening to me, like I said earlier, we could fight!

Faith said, "Maddie is right, I think we should ask Mrs. T first, before we get too ahead of ourselves."

The evening was done for the group, and everyone went home.

The next day was the same routine in the morning for the four friends while going to school. Class went on as usual, however this time there was more discussion on the cutting down of the tree.

As they were in class, they brought up their concerns to Mrs. T, they also brought up their solutions to Mrs. T.

Hunter asked, "so, which would you pick, Mrs. T my idea right?" I say let's show them we're strong.

Mrs. T responded, "that's an interesting idea, and it shows that you have the determination, but.... Hunter, is there another way that can show that we are determined and strong without so much of a hard approach and something everyone might be willing to participate with?" -Class can I have your attention?" Our task for today is choosing which ideas we heard are best for the Tree of Sacrifice to be saved. We'll write it down, pass it forward, and vote on it, separate sheets of paper of course, and this concerns everyone who wants to participate. You can express your own ideas, or leave it blank as well.

All ideas were interesting. Fighting being one, protest being another, and some that went as far as hiding the tree. But one idea which Mrs. T found more sensible, and involved was the petition idea, submitted by Faith. So, they voted, and Faith's idea standed out the most, which was the petition.

Mason said…. "I still think we should fight!" After Mason said that, the class began to talk loudly and argue, and everything.

(look at this guy, everything was starting to move forward and he got them all riled up.   -Mason, slow down a minute, let's hear this one out, they are still discussing it, remember. (((whew)))

Mrs. T says to the class,

"Listen up everybody, there is more than one way to fight a battle. There's more than one way to express a difference of opinions, and there's more than one way to show that you are strong in your task. Class a solution for this is that one has to decide which is the correct route, to get the best results of a situation, at the right time from the problem at hand being debated or being questioned.

The class listened to Mrs. T's teachings and continued with their project to save the tree. As their journey was to continue, Mrs. T gave them all the information they needed to pursue the signatures for the petition.

Going through the rest of the week, the four friends worked around the clock to get as many signatures as they could, including their own. They made more flyers, more posters, even their parents spread the word at work.

(As you can see those students were serious, and they didn't give up)

By Friday, they had 300 signatures on the petition, which was in the guidelines Mrs. T had given them earlier that week.

Mrs. T quieted them down in the class just to have them normalizing the day. Unaware of the next step of their accomplishments, she surprised them with an unexpected early move.

Mrs. T says, "Class please everyone, may I have your full attention. We have come so far to realize that we have reached our goal of signatures on the petition, now, let's go save the Tree of Sacrifice.

The class cheered as they heard those words come out of Mrs. T's mouth, they were so excited by the news that they may be able to see the tree still standing. Mrs. T, once again, had to quiet them down because they were getting even louder, and at that time, they needed to stay safe, follow instructions, pack their stuff, and head for the bus to the Tree of Sacrifice. Mrs. T had the transportation already there because she knew and pre planned their exit. All the kids boarded the school bus for the trip, they were on their way to the park.

They arrived at the destination. It was a short trip, but, for the students and the teacher, with all the excitement and all the anticipation, and all the nervousness, and all the everything, it seemed like it took another week or two.

"Wow," Maddie whispered, "the Tree of Sacrifice is huge."
"Yeah," Mason said. "But let's hope our signatures are BIG enough to save it."

Faith said, "yeah, we followed all the rules, we just have to make it there in time.

Mason added. "If we are not there in time my offer still stands." Even Vallery had a little change of heart because of the choices they made, so she chimed in and said, "Mason, knock it off!"

Hunter said, "way to go, Vallery, a change of heart!"

Vallery responded, "Well, I do feel a little good about what we did, it felt like I had a voice, and it was important. I mean, is that ok with y'all?"

Maddie said... "hey Vallery, thanks for participating, and yeah, that's real cool"

Vallery said.... "Thanks, Maddie, I guess, maybe you aren't as bad as I thought you were. I guess it's better to let people speak for themselves before I speak for them. Unless, you know, they're scared to talk, and then I'll talk for them."

(Yeah, Vallery! That's what I'm talking about. See, people can change)

The class saw the workers gathered around the tree, with caution tape, rapping around the area. Other people from around the city were there as well, to witness the Tree of Sacrifice be cut down. The equipment was ready, and the workers were about to begin the set up process of their ordered agenda when the teacher, other adults, and the four friends leading the class behind, ran over to the site. Mason held up a sign that said, "SAVE THE TREE," he started marching around the tree and shouting, "LEAVE IT ALONE!!" "LEAVE IT ALONE, GO AWAY, WE DON'T WANT YOU HERE, WHAT? YOU WANT TO FIGHT!!"

He turned to everyone in the group and said, "I think it's too late, we might as well start our attack while we have them off guard!"

Maddie turned around and looked at Mason, "WHAT, WHOA, WHO, Wait a minute, not now dude. Hold up, let's try what we worked for first!"

Vallery chimed in as she shoved Maddie out the way, "I'm in with you Mason, just because y'all don't like the tree, doesn't mean you speak for everybody!"

The other three ran up to the workers and showed them the completed, signed, petition with all the signatures they needed for the tree to be saved. The workers read all the signatures on the petition, and as they began to talk about it, they were impressed and had no choice but to leave the tree of sacrifice alone. The class cheered with happiness and hugged each other.

"We did it!" Maddie cheered as she hugged Mason.

"Hmm, well, I guess this tree isn't that bad looking after all," Vallery said as she smirked looking around at everybody.

(oh Vallery, simple Vallery, only you can say something like that at this point of the story)

Vallery said to the narrator, "Yeah narrator, I still have to keep up my image, I can't show people that I'm getting soft."

(Vallery, your stronger than you think you are, keep fighting for the right reasons)

Faith and Hunter hung the petition on the front of the tree, so if anyone attempts to cut down the Tree of Sacrifice again, they're going to have to understand and recognize that people like this tree, want it here, and have made a point that they are willing to stand for the continuation of the tree. They will know that the Tree of Sacrifice is too important and has too much history that helped generations sprout into free thinking strong people that proved the purpose is worth the degree it stood for. Our rights of passage, a change of direction, a way of productive, positive thinking, it stood there with its decency and dignity it did not fight, it did not move, it did not speak because it couldn't but the people showed it was worth keeping by representing peacefulness with their solution.

Printed in the United States
by Baker & Taylor Publisher Services